This book belongs to

..................................................................................................

# AUTUMN
## PUBLISHING

Published in 2019
by Autumn Publishing
Cottage Farm
Sywell
NN6 0BJ
www.autumnpublishing.co.uk

1219 001
2 4 6 8 10 9 7 5 3 1
ISBN 978-1-83852-729-7

Illustrated by James Newman Gray
Written by Marnie Willow

Cover designed by Nicholas Gage and Lee Italiano
Interiors designed by Lee Italiano

Edited by Helen Catt

Printed and manufactured in China

# My First Day of School

AUTUMN
PUBLISHING

I go to school tomorrow. Mom says it will be fun.

But all the big kids go there, and I think I'm too young.

I'm sure that I'm not ready, I don't know what to bring.

Mom says she has a list so we remember everything.

But I'm still not feeling ready.
It's a long, long way to go.

The bus driver might forget the
way and get us lost, you know!

Mom says the driver knows the way.
He's never been lost before.

I say there's a first
time for everything,
so how can you
be sure?

Bear says I can hold her paw, and she'll sit next to me.

She says, "School isn't scary. We'll have fun, you'll see!"

What if the teacher never smiles? What if he's grumpy and mean?

But when we see him, he smiles and waves. "Hello! I'm Mr. Green."

Mr. Green knows
all our names.
He knows I'm
great at art.

He knows that Bear
is my best friend,
and that she's
really smart.

First we sit, criss-cross applesauce,
for circle-time together.

We talk about the calendar,
the day and month and weather.

Then it's time to do some math.
We play a counting game.

Next we do some ABCs. I even write my name.

Next I draw a **dinosaur**...

... in a

**Silly
hat.**

Bear knocks over all the paints...

... and makes a great BIG splat!

At lunchtime, **I can't wait** to see what Mom's packed in **my box**...

... my favorite **yummy** sandwich and some treats I **share** with Fox.

Then we go outside to **play**.

I climb up really **high**.

I slide down with a **whizz** and **"Whee!"**

while Bear swings **up** to the sky.

Mr. Green calls us inside and says,

"It's story time."

"I have a special **book** to read, with a **very funny** rhyme."

There are **pigs** in **wigs**...

... and **frogs** in **clogs**...

... and a **shrew** with just one **shoe**.

**Bears** on **stairs** and **baboons** with **spoons**...

... it's a **very silly zoo**.

When **toy time** comes, I build a **shop**.
It sells **amazing** toys.

I pack them **all** in **paper** bags,
And **count** out **all** the coins.

Then **suddenly** it's time to go.
We all get on the bus.

When
we get home,
Mom's waiting.
I say, "Mom, don't
make a fuss."

"I'm a **schoolkid** now, you see,
I'm too grown up for this."

Mom laughs at me (I don't know why)
and gives me a **great big kiss.**